MW01049904

Are You Flying, Charlie Duncan?

Are You Flying, Charlie Duncan?

Elizabeth Lee O'Donnell

ILLUSTRATED BY

Karen Milone

MORROW JUNIOR BOOKS

New York

Inquiries should be addressed to William Morrow
and Company, Inc.,
1350 Avenue of the Americas, New York, N.Y. 10019.
Printed in the United States of America.
1   2   3   4   5   6   7   8   9   10

Library of Congress Cataloging-in-Publication Data
O'Donnell, Elizabeth Lee.   Are you flying, Charlie Duncan? /
Elizabeth Lee O'Donnell : illustrated by
Karen Milone.   p.   cm.
Summary: A shy ten-year-old learns to stand his ground after
discovering that he is half boy, half balloon.
ISBN 0-688-09027-3   [1. Balloons—Fiction.   2. Assertiveness
(Psychology)—Fiction.]   I. Milone-Dugan, Karen, ill.
II. Title.   PZ7.02244Ar   1993   [Fic]—dc20
92-39876   CIP   AC

For Jo Cooper and David Duisberg
—E. L. O'D.

Contents

1	Circus	1
2	Sticks and Stones	10
3	A Green Visitor	1
4	Soccer Team	31
5	Charlie's Secret Place	38
6	One Question Too Many	4
7	One Answer Too Many	60
8	Brunhilda	70
9	A Rough Ride . . .	84
10	. . . And a Rougher Landing	92
11	Green at Last	99
12	Grounded	109
13	Part of a Pride	117
14	Winners	126

Are You Flying, Charlie Duncan?

1

Circus

The Thursday before school opened, every kid in town was watching the circus elephants slosh water.

Every kid but one.

Charlie Duncan was under his bed.

It wasn't the place he'd planned to spend this Thursday morning. He'd gotten up just before dawn as usual. The kitchen was night dark, but Charlie didn't need lights. He spilled cereal and milk into a bowl, shoved a spoon into his pocket, and slipped out the back door. He sat on the high porch rail and held his breath.

There it was! The sun peeked over the edge of

the world. Seeing it like that, just a tiny bit of it showing, made his stomach feel like it had the giggles. Charlie spooned up cereal and watched the sun float upward like a big yellow balloon.

He finished his cereal and sighed happily. It was going to be another good day. The circus was in town, and where there was a circus, there would be balloons. Charlie couldn't remember a time when balloons weren't important to him. He always knew they were special. Magical almost.

He grinned. "Soon," he whispered to the morning breeze. "I'll be there soon." He ducked back into the house to do his morning chores.

At eight-thirty Charlie charged downstairs for a second breakfast. Mom always fixed iced cocoa during August. As he rounded the corner leading to the kitchen, he heard Mom and Kate talking. Blast! He was sure Kate would still be in bed. He tiptoed to the door and looked through the crack.

"Well, Katie, if you really want to take Charlie, I suppose it's all right. But I don't think Charlie likes slugs much."

"Oh, Mom," Kate moaned. "I'm not going after slugs. Just pond samples. I want to have a

2

great exhibit for the science fair this year, and—"

"And Charlie's not interested," Mom cut in.

"Oh, Mom! He should be! He's in *fifth* grade now. Can't you *make* him come? Besides, I need somebody to help carry junk— I mean my equipment."

Mom shook her head and reached for her purse. "Why should I, Katie, my darlin'? He's happy doing whatever it is he does."

"How can you say that? He never does *anything* with *anybody*!"

Mom raised her eyebrows.

"Well, he doesn't," said Kate. "You don't under—"

"Katherine Marie! Don't you dare tell me one more time that I don't understand! Maybe I don't, but I doubt you do either. And I have to get going or I'll be late for work."

Kate was still muttering as Charlie headed back upstairs. He looked around his room for a hiding place. He had no intention of being Kate's pack mule. If he took time to argue with her, he'd be late for the circus.

Charlie looked at his bed. "That'll do it," he

muttered. He smoothed out his sheet, pulled up the light summer spread, and wiggled under the bed. With luck, Kate would think he'd already slipped out of the house.

As the minutes ticked by, Charlie stared at the loose cheesecloth stuff above him. Where does all the dust come from? he wondered. Mom made him vacuum twice a week.

"Where is she?" Charlie fumed under his breath. "It's hot under here." How much dust would there be if he didn't vacuum? Who cares? And who cared what Kate thought? Mom was right: He was happy. Something nudged at his mind. I am too happy! he snapped at the stray thought. Just because I don't hang around with a lot of guys . . .

He heard Kate pounding up the stairs.

"Charlie! Hey, *Charlie*! Where are you? Mom said I should take you with me. Hey, Charlie!"

His door slammed open. Charlie held his breath. What a liar! he thought. "Mom said," my foot!

"Charlie? Are you hiding, Charlie?"

Charlie heard her open his closet. Then she sat on his bed. Dust floated.

I'll sneeze, Charlie thought, and pinched his nose.

Kate jumped up. "That Charlie! I bet he snuck out the back." She slammed his door so hard, it bounced back open.

Under the bed, Charlie grinned. That took care of that. He inched his way out and dusted himself off.

"Money," he muttered. "I'll need some money." He upended his hedgehog bank and picked out all the quarters.

Charlie was halfway down the stairs when Kate's voice bashed against his ears.

"You come back here, Charlie Duncan!"

Charlie flapped a hand at her and kept going.

"You're supposed to help me with my experiments!" she yelled.

He banged through the front door.

"I know where you're going! That stupid circus! It's a *nothing* of a circus! Everybody knows that! I bet they don't even have *elephants!*"

Her voice chased him down the block.

"A lot she knows!" he told the grass as he jogged along. "All the posters said there were elephants!"

5

As he entered the fairgrounds, Charlie made a face. He really hated it when Kate was right. Jupiter's Splendiferous Super Stupendous Circus wasn't very big, even if there were elephants. The big top—yellow and green stripes instead of red and white—had only a single pole. It can't hold a lot of people, he thought.

A cheer roared out of the tent.

Charlie grinned. Quality, he thought. Just like Mom says, it's quality, not quantity, that counts.

The midway was small too, but it had all the right things for a circus. Flags of all sizes blew and snapped in the hot breeze. Wagons decked out with swirls and spangles and colored lights were backdrops for the shouting barkers. *"Step right up, ladies and gentlemen! Only one thin quarter for three balls! Step right up!"* And the smells! Mustard and dust, straw and snow cones. Hot dogs and . . .

Suddenly Charlie was starving. That cereal had been a long time ago. He fumbled in his pocket for his quarters.

Taking big bites out of a foot-long hot dog, Charlie looked around for the balloon seller. He heard a high squeak and a pop. That was the throw-the-dart booth. That wasn't what he wanted. Where . . . ?

There he was.

"Bal-looonnnsss!" the man yelled. "Round ones, skinny ones, big fat double ones! Red ones, orange ones! Blue, green, and purple ones! *Bal-looonnnsss!"*

Charlie gulped down the last of his hot dog and wiped his hands on his jeans.

Just look at them! he thought. Something inside him jumped, and his heart thudded wildly. All those balloons! There must be fifty or a hundred, their strings so tangled, it was a wonder they could ever be separated.

Charlie trailed along after the balloon man. The balloons strained against their strings. Most of them were just regular balloons, but some of them were what Charlie called *special*.

An Orange smirked at him. Charlie shook his head. A long Red looked just like Kate. Not that one either. A small Yellow sniffed and bobbed away.

What if there wasn't one that was his kind of special? Impossible, thought Charlie. But as he dogged the balloon man's steps, he began to wonder. Maybe this time he'd come up empty.

7

Just then a fat, green, tear-shaped balloon poked itself out of the middle of the group. It bounced around a bit and then settled lower and lower, as if it were losing helium.

Charlie nodded and reached into his pocket for his quarters. "Hey, mister! I'd like that one," he said, pointing to the drifting Green.

The balloon man twirled the balloons around and around. "This one?" he asked, pulling at the string of a dark blue one.

"No, sir," said Charlie. "*That* one!"

"But it's losing air, son. It'll be flat before you can say Jack Robinson."

"That's okay. That's the one I want."

The balloon man shrugged and untangled the green balloon from the rest. "You can't get your money back, you know."

"I know. But it's okay." Charlie reached out for the balloon. "Honest. It's okay!" He handed over his money and wrapped the balloon's string loosely around his wrist. "Thanks."

Charlie walked toward the big top. He grinned up at the balloon. "Hi," he said.

"Hiya, kid!" said the balloon. "How ya doin'?"

2

Sticks and Stones

The balloon pulled on Charlie's wrist. "Where you going, kid?"

"Thought we'd see the show," said Charlie.

"Too late. Only one show today. Mr. Spanovich overbooked. We have to upstake early or forfeit our advance."

"What?"

Green chuckled. "Circus talk. Mr. S. booked us into Danville for tomorrow, so we have to pack up and move this afternoon. Otherwise, we have to give Danville back the money they gave us in advance."

"Oh," said Charlie. "Who's Mr. Spanovich?"

"He owns the circus."

"I thought it was somebody named Jupiter."

"Old Henry B. Jupiter started it—oh, a hundred years ago or so. Circuses mostly keep the same name no matter who comes on board."

"Oh," Charlie said again. "Was it— I mean, is it a good show?"

"Not bad, kid, not bad. But sometimes the show *inside* the show is better."

"What do you mean?" asked Charlie.

The green balloon bounced up and down. "You should see it when the LaVoie brothers— they're the acrobats—get into fights! They roll and bounce and flip from one end of the pitch to the other."

"The pitch?"

"The grounds, kid. The midway."

Charlie squinted down the midway as though trying to picture the fight. "Must be something," he said, and wiped his face with the tail of his T-shirt.

The balloon looked Charlie up and down. "You look hot, kid. Why don't you give Jack a little business?"

"Is that him?" Charlie nodded toward a soft-drink booth.

"Right."

Charlie wandered over toward the booth. "Don't you get hot?"

"Uh-uh," said the balloon. "With the breeze up here, it ain't so bad. And being a circus balloon, you get used to the heat. We're out day after day—and usually at the hottest part of the day. Course, sometimes we get out after dark. I like it then. Warm, you know, but not what you'd call hot."

The balloon talked on as Charlie got his lemonade—with extra ice—and talked on as he drank it. Charlie was looking at the posters of the trapeze act when the balloon suddenly stopped talking.

"What's the matter?" Charlie asked.

"You aren't saying much," said the balloon.

Charlie shrugged. None of the other balloons he'd talked to had ever asked him about himself. Usually the balloons just chatted on about places they'd seen or places they wanted to see. What could he talk about? "I'm going to try out for the soccer team," he said. "Dad says it'll be good exercise." That wasn't exactly what Dad said, but what the heck. What would this balloon care if the exercise Dad meant was in talking to people and making friends? "I read a lot." What else did he do? Charlie suddenly wondered if Kate had a point.

"Books?" said the balloon.

Charlie nodded. "I've got some really good ones."

"At your pitch?"

"Do you want to see them?" Charlie was surprised.

Green looked uncomfortable. "Well, yeah. I've never really seen one close up. Heard about them though. A cousin of mine worked this school fair. He said they were beautiful."

"I'd be happy to show you my books," said Charlie. "If we can avoid my sister."

"Bigger or littler?"

"Bigger."

"They can be a pain, kid. I know. Now me— well, I guess I'm just lucky. No sisters. Lots of brothers and a bunch of cousins. But I've done a sort of study. Trust me, kid. Little ones are worse.

"Hey!" the balloon yelped. "Did you see that?"

"What?"

"That kid! That pie-faced one over there. He's got a slingshot. A rock just missed me!"

Charlie looked around. Blast! It was Sam Baker. Charlie had managed to avoid him all summer.

Sam had heckled Charlie through the whole of fourth grade. When Charlie went to the drinking fountain, Sam's foot just "happened" to be in the aisle. The few times Charlie had tried to join in the sockball or handball games, there was Sam: "Don't choose Charlie. He'll only louse us up. He's a total klutz."

And so, of course, Charlie became the klutz Sam said he was. He tripped over his own feet, slipped on a patch of dirt, missed hitting or catching the ball by a mile.

And here was Sam! Big as King Kong and twice as ugly. "We'd better head home," said Charlie, and tugged at the balloon's string.

"Hey, Charlie!" Sam called. "Has the little boy got his pretty balloon?" His voice was loud, sneery.

Dumb jerk! Charlie yelled at himself. Why

14

can't I ever think of anything to say back? He trotted toward the exit.

Out of the corner of his eye, Charlie saw Sam move. The slingshot came up. Charlie flicked the balloon string off his wrist.

"Go!" he yelled.

The rock missed the balloon by more than a foot, but Charlie flinched and dropped to the ground. That dumb rock had missed his ear by an inch—or less.

Sam looked around—casually—to see how many people were watching.

A lot, Charlie noticed.

"Too bad!" Sam yelled at him. "The little boy's lost his pretty toy!"

Charlie stood up and brushed himself off. A little more dirt didn't matter, but he hated looking like a wimp. What if somebody he knew had seen? He swallowed hard. Of course, he said to himself. The show *would* have to let out now. Three boys from his class stood just outside the main tent.

Mark Richards, who played soccer in season and out, looked naked without his soccer ball. Joseph Hammersmith, Mark's best friend, had his hands buried deep in his pockets as usual.

15

He lifted his chin at Charlie. Girard LeMon smiled and half waved. Girard had arrived from France the last week in May.

The three boys strolled over to him. Maybe, Charlie hoped, they hadn't seen him sprawled in the dirt.

"Hi," said Mark. "Did you see the show?"

Charlie shook his head. Why couldn't he find *something* to say to people! He began to back away.

"Well show!" said Girard. "I like much."

" 'Good' show," said Joseph. "I'm helping Girard with his English," he explained.

"Oh," said Charlie. He took another step back.

Sam joined them, tucking his slingshot into a back pocket. "Leaving, Charlie?"

"I've got stuff to do."

"For Mommy?"

Charlie missed the look Mark and Joseph exchanged. His ears were burning, and he was concentrating on not looking at the ground. Dad said you should always keep your head up, no matter what.

"Charlie missed the show," Sam told the others. "He was too busy buying a balloon to play with."

"Maybe he likes balloons," said Joseph in his soft way.

"Too bad then," said Sam. "There it goes."

The green balloon was still traveling up. It looked bright against the blue sky.

"Poor little Charlie will just have to buy another one."

Charlie shrugged. "Yeah. I guess. See you, guys."

Joseph pointed his chin at Charlie. "Tryouts for the soccer team Saturday, Charlie. You coming?"

Charlie nodded.

"I don't know why," sniped Sam. "You'll never make it."

Charlie lifted a hand and headed for the exit. He had had enough.

"But your balloon!" taunted Sam.

Charlie half turned, opened his mouth, but couldn't think of anything to say. He turned back and walked on.

He heard Mark say something. It sounded like "Leave it be," but Charlie wasn't sure. What he heard loud as a trumpet was Sam's "Is he for real?"

Sam's voice crawled up the back of his neck,

but Charlie kept on walking. "I'm real enough," he told the fence as he passed it. "Just a different real. Sometimes, though, I wish I were regular real. Maybe then I'd know what to say to the guys. Maybe even how to stop Sam's mouth." He jogged on. After about half a mile, he began to watch the sky. No sign of the green balloon. Maybe . . .

"Boo!" The green balloon popped out from behind a tree. "Did I scare you?"

"A little," said Charlie so he wouldn't hurt the balloon's feelings. "Where'd you go?"

"Up yonder. Up along. High in the sky."

Charlie grinned. "You sure can move when you have to."

The balloon bobbed up and down. "Right! You gotta be fast to work in a circus, kid. You did invite me home, didn't you?"

"Right," said Charlie. "It's this way." He pointed up the block.

"Good-o, kid. That's Australian talk. A juggler from Sydney joined up last year. I could use a little rest. Ducking rocks is tiring!" The balloon kept pace with Charlie, dangling by his left ear. "Say! What's with that pie-faced kid? He's a real loser."

Charlie didn't have to answer because the balloon went on talking.

"Before we were so rudely interrupted by that jerk, I was telling you about my cousin who works book fairs. Or would you rather hear about Leathers, the juggler from Down Under?"

3

A Green Visitor

The green balloon bobbed around the walls in Charlie's room. He stopped in front of a huge poster. "This is nice, kid."

Charlie, squatting by his bookcase, looked over his shoulder.

"I like it," the balloon said. "It's better than any of our posters. Even the one for the lion act."

"My Dad got it for me. It's a hot-air balloon meet. Are you related to them?" He pulled books from the middle shelf and piled them on the bed.

"Sort of." Green drifted over to Charlie's bed. "Wow! You sure got a lot of books!"

Charlie grinned and pulled more books.

"Have you read them all?"

"Not really. With some, I just look at the pictures." He pulled *Treasure Island* from under the pile. "Like this one. It's hard to read, so I find a picture and then read the bits about it."

"*That* makes me feel better!" said the balloon. "I was beginning to think I was a real dummy. Here I am, hardly ever reading *anything,* and there you are reading *everything*!" He bobbed up and down over the pile of books.

"Well," said Charlie uncomfortably, "you probably don't get much chance to read at the circus."

"How right you are, kid! Now, my cousin, the book-fair one, reads a lot. When I run into him, he always has a new favorite. What's your favorite out of this mess?"

"That's hard," said Charlie. He turned books over. "I kind of like the ones about kids who take charge. And the ones about dragons. And the ones about magic. And the ones—"

"What's that one?" the balloon asked.

"*Dragon Magic.* It's really good. Want to hear it?"

"You already read it."

"That's okay. I always read the best ones at least twice." Charlie shoved all the books to the foot of the bed. He kicked off his shoes and wiggled himself into a comfortable position. "You won't laugh if I pronounce some of the words wrong, will you?"

"Course not!"

"Okay then. Ready?"

"Ready," said the balloon. He dangled himself behind Charlie's left ear.

Charlie opened the book. " 'Dragon Magic,' " he read, "by Andre Norton. Chapter One— Hidden Treasure. Sig Dortmund kicked at a pile of leaves . . ."

They were deep in Chapter Two, the one about the dragon Fafnir, when Dad's voice drifted up the stairs and snuck under Charlie's closed door.

"Dinner! Come get it or I'll feed the cats!"

"That your dad?"

Charlie nodded.

The balloon tilted himself as though listening. "He sounds okay. I'll bet he works outside."

"He does," said Charlie, closing the book.

"He's a gardener. Can you *hear* how people are? What they do?"

"Most of the time. We're up so high, you know. What can you tell by the top of some-body's head? But you can hear all kinds of things in voices. Your dad's is . . ."—he bobbed up and down—". . . is meadow-warm. Like September at dusk. Or the outback of the circus. But some voices are pin-sharp or shrill-mean. Some are furry. Some are slickery. Some . . ."

Charlie edged toward his door. If he didn't get downstairs, Dad's voice might change into lion-on-the-hunt warm. "Would you like to come down for dinner?" Charlie cut in as politely as he could.

Never having had a balloon come home with him before, he wasn't sure what he should do. Mom said you always ask visitors to eat. But do balloons eat? he wondered. And introducing him might be a problem. Charlie doubted that anyone else in his family talked with balloons. Once Kate had been standing at his elbow when a fat Purple yelled, "Race you to the tree!" She didn't seem to hear him. Dad talked to plants, but he'd never mentioned that they talked back.

25

And Mom only muttered at carrots and cheese and other stuff.

But the balloon didn't want dinner. "I don't think so, kid," he said. "If it's okay by you, I'll dip through some more of your books. The picture ones. If you'll spread them out."

"Sure." Charlie pulled all his picture books off the bottom shelf of his bookcase and spread them around the bed and desk. He left the balloon dangling over the bed, dipping and swaying slightly from the evening breeze.

"Your turn to say grace, Charlie," Mom said as he slid into his seat.

Charlie bowed his head. "Thank you, God, for the food on our table, especially the mashed potatoes. Thank you for today, for yesterday, and for the surprises of tomorrow."

Kate glared at him. "Mom, he *never* does it right!"

"It was a nice grace though," Dad said. "Charlie has an original turn of mind. And since it was my turn to cook, I appreciate the thought."

"But it's not right!" Kate said stubbornly.

Charlie looked at Dad. "Should I do it over?"

"No, Charlie. It was fine."

"I thought so," said Charlie. He reached for the brussels sprouts.

"See, Mom," Kate got in. "He even likes *those* things."

"I wish you did," Mom said.

"Charlie wouldn't come with me to get pond samples."

Charlie looked up from his plate. "Nobody said I had to."

"Mom said . . ."

Mom put down her coffee cup. "I did not. And you know it."

"What *did* you do today, Charlie?" asked Dad.

"Circus," he said around a mouthful of brussels sprouts.

"That's right," said Mom. "I remember, now. How was the show?"

"I missed it. I wandered around the midway."

Dad looked at Mom. They both looked at Kate. She was suddenly very busy cutting her meat loaf.

"Katherine Marie!" said Mom. "Did you have anything to do with Charlie missing the circus?"

"Oh, Mo-om!" Kate made "Mom" two syllables.

"Did you?"

27

"I never even *saw* Charlie!"

What a liar, thought Charlie, and wondered if he should mention the fact that he spent a lot of time under his bed. No, he decided. I might need it as a hiding place again.

"As a matter of fact, I wasted a lot of time looking for him. I was *late*! Mary waited and *waited* for me. *Her* little brother helped carry her stuff. Mary says Charlie ought to get his nose out of a book once in a while, be more *helpful*. . . ."

Charlie made a nest in his mashed potatoes. Kate's voice went on and on. What would Green think of her voice? he wondered. "May I have the gravy?" he asked.

"Charlie," said Mom as she handed him the gravy bowl. "Why do you just sit there? You *do* do things."

"Kate doesn't think what I do is anything. Maybe if I get on the soccer team, she can come to some of my games. Or I could read her a book."

"Oh, Mother! I don't *want*—"

"That's enough, Kate. And speaking of soccer," Mom went on, "save Saturday for me. If it's time for soccer, it's time for school to start. You both need some things to start the year."

"The tryouts are at one o'clock."

Mom nodded. "That's all right. We can do you first."

"But I wanted to—" That's as far as Kate got.

"Katherine Marie. This Saturday is my Saturday off." Mom worked at the library in the research department.

Dad winked at Charlie. "It's called democracy, Katie. Do it Saturday or go back to school with last year's clothes. Your choice."

"Oh, Daddy! I need new jeans and running shoes and . . ."

"May I be excused?" Charlie asked.

"It's your turn to do dishes!" Kate snapped.

"I forgot."

Mom and Dad looked at each other again. "I think you might offer to take Charlie's place," said Mom.

"Me-e?" Kate made that two syllables too. "Why should I do *his* dishes?"

"The circus doesn't come to town all that often," Dad said mildly.

"Oh," said Kate. She bit her lip and took a

deep breath. "I'll do the dishes tonight, Charlie. I'm sorry you missed the circus."

Charlie shoved his chair back. "That's okay," he said. "I'll help." If only she hadn't apologized, he wouldn't have had to do the dishes. That was the trouble with Kate: She'd do all this dumb stuff, and at the last minute she'd turn nice.

4

Soccer Team

"I hamf tum um fimmin ther," Charlie said on Saturday morning.

" 'Hamf tum um fimmin ther'?" said the balloon.

Charlie pulled his T-shirt clear of his face. "Sorry. I said: I have to go with my mother. To get stuff for school. Want to come?"

"I went shopping once. Didn't like it much."

"I don't like it much either," said Charlie. "But Mom likes me to try on all the stuff. And then I've got to go to the soccer tryouts. And if I make the team, there's practice."

"Is that the game you told me about?" asked

the balloon. "Where you don't use your hands?"

"Right. Only you do sometimes."

"I remember. You use your head."

"And feet," said Charlie.

"That sounds like something I'd like to see."

Charlie gave him directions to the park where the team practiced. "See you there at one," he said. He left the balloon skimming through a yellow-jacketed picture book. Charlie had been impressed by how fast Green had learned to turn pages by using his string and whatever breeze drifted in the open window.

At five minutes to one, Charlie jogged into the park. Boy! Was he ever glad *that* was over! He didn't mind shopping with Mom, but with Kate—ugh!

He'd seen Mark at the shoe store, Joseph and Girard at the stationery store. But he'd only half waved at them. What could he say? "Didn't we have a great time at the circus?" Or maybe, "Come on over to my house and meet my friend, Green."

Get real! Charlie snapped at himself.

Charlie looked around for the balloon. Not many places for a balloon to hide, he thought. Then he heard a sort of humming.

"He flies through the air
with the greatest of ease,
that daring young man on
the flying trapeze."

Charlie grinned and trotted toward the far end of the field. There'd been times he was sorry he'd ever offered to read to Green. He'd read till his throat was raw, but the balloon had really liked it. And had paid him back by telling stories and singing songs Charlie had never heard before.

He stood under the old sycamore and looked up. "Hi!" he called. "I thought I heard you."

The balloon was on the far side of the tree, high up in the branches. "Hiya, kid. Thought I saw that twerp with the slingshot, so I hid up here. Those dragon boys would take care of him soon enough."

"They would at that," said Charlie, and wished he was one of them. And I wish we were home reading now, he thought. His stomach was doing peculiar things. He glanced toward the field. There were an awful lot of kids there, including Sam Baker. He should have known Sam would try out. Maybe he could just tell Dad he hadn't made the team, and then—

33

"Are they starting now, kid?"

"Yeah, I guess so. Can you see okay from up there?"

"Aye, that I can! As dragon boy Artie might say."

"See you later then," said Charlie, and walked toward the big group of kids. With Green watching, he'd have to go through with it.

He stood at the edge of the group. Coach Tyler was sorting everybody out. Over half the kids were in the wrong part of the park. The Jordan County Soccer League was divided into age groups. Only the ten- and eleven-year-olds were supposed to be here. Other groups were supposed to meet in different parts of the park.

"Over there!" Coach Tyler kept shouting.

By the time everyone had scattered to the proper place, there were fifteen kids left standing in front of Coach Tyler. That was four more than was needed on an eleven-person team. Charlie figured he could just go on home and tell Dad he hadn't made it.

But it didn't work out that way. Before he could back quietly out of sight, Coach Tyler sent him out with Joseph to run passes down the field.

Well, Charlie thought to himself, here goes nothing. But with Green watching, he would try his best—even if it wasn't much.

Charlie surprised himself by being pretty good at it. No matter where Joseph put the ball, Charlie could "see" the angle and be there to get it. Sometimes he forgot all about Green and just enjoyed the taste of doing something right for once.

Joseph nodded at him as they jogged back to Coach Tyler. "Not shabby," he said quietly.

Charlie couldn't think of anything to say. He tried things in his mind. *Oh, that was nothing.* No. *I tried hard.* No. *Maybe I've got an aptitude for it.* No. *I think I need more practice.* That was more like it.

A voice at his elbow startled him. "Probably comes from chasing balloons," sneered Sam.

"Doesn't matter," said Joseph. "He gets there."

"It's only a practice. I bet you were easy on him."

Joseph shrugged.

Charlie felt like he wasn't there. He slowed his steps to let the other boys go on ahead. Had Joseph been easy on him? It hadn't felt like it, but Charlie had never played soccer before. What did he know?

At the end of an hour, Coach announced that everyone who tried out was on the team. Four of the boys were alternates, but Charlie was chosen starting sweeper. Mark slapped him on the back, but Charlie still couldn't think of anything to say.

Well, he thought as he walked over to the sycamore to collect Green, at least Dad will be glad. And maybe Kate *will* have to come to one of my games. That made him smile.

The balloon wasn't there. Charlie looked all around the park. "Maybe he'll pop out at me on the way home," he told a fading rosebush.

But no balloon popped out to scare him. And his room was empty. The only trace of his visitor was the books scattered all over.

Charlie sighed and picked up *Dragon Magic*. Green had been the first balloon who'd ever come home with him. Before, they'd just bobbed along with him for a while, and then they'd gone off on their own business. "I guess," said Charlie to the book, "I thought he'd stay longer." He shoved books back into the bookcase. "I wish he

36

had. He never finished that story about the clown who wanted to fly on the trapeze."

Life would seem awfully dull without old Green. He swallowed hard. Empty, too. It had been kind of nice having a friend over.

But maybe Dad was right; maybe being on the soccer team would give him some friends. Maybe he'd even ask Joseph to come over one afternoon after practice.

5

Charlie's Secret Place

The Thursday before Thanksgiving, every kid in Charlie's class scattered by twos and threes.

Every kid but one.

Charlie scuffed through the autumn leaves by himself. It had been another one of those days. "Blast!" he muttered at every step. "Blast!"

Just beyond the Brickle Salvage Yard office, Charlie counted boards in the fence. ". . . seven, eight, nine!" He pushed on the loose one and slid through. There'd been a lot of terrible days since school opened. Too many.

Charlie threaded his way through the yard.

He thought of it as the Brickle Obstacle Course because it usually took a long time to get to the other end. Who could just walk by those splintery sea chests? Or the trunks of secrets guarded by rusted locks? Or the mysterious black boxes that nested one inside the other? It was even hard to pass the barrels of bent nails, the wood-burning stoves and iceboxes, the crumbling magazines in mouse-gnawed crates.

But today Charlie made a beeline for the back wall and a huge packing box. Once it had held a piano. Now an old tarp covered one end.

Charlie pushed the tarp aside, tossed his spelling book in a corner, and sat down. He shoved a couple of mildewed cushions behind his back and wrapped his arms around his knees. How could anybody be in so much trouble when he hadn't *done* anything?

He rocked back and forth. And stopped. An almost smile tilted one corner of his mouth. A thermos stood on the orange crate he used for a table. Steam rose as Charlie took off the lid. The chocolate smell made his mouth water.

You can never tell about Mr. Brickle, he thought, and reached for the cup. Charlie had first snuck into the yard over a year ago. When he'd met Mr. Brickle coming around an old stove, Charlie thought he'd be thrown out. But the old man had held out his hand. "I'm Earl Brickle," he said, shaking Charlie's hand. "I own all this. More fun to sneak in, but if you want, you can come in by the front." Mr. Brickle had lifted his chin toward the back. "You might look over that way. Thought maybe somebody could find a use for that old crate."

"That old crate" had become Charlie's own place, his secret place. Since then Charlie had discovered that Mr. Brickle's temper was uncertain. Sometimes he'd walk around with Charlie, pointing out his choicest treasures. Other times he'd kind of growl, mutter about "danged nuisances," and disappear into his office.

But Charlie had noticed that often, when he'd had a really bad day, Mr. Brickle would leave little surprises for him. Just after Green disappeared, Mr. Brickle had left a thermos of ice-cold lemonade. After that first, disastrous soccer game, there had been cold milk and cake. Then apple cider, candy apples, popcorn. And now hot chocolate. But every time Charlie thanked him, Mr. Brickle shook his head.

"Don't think on it, Charlie Duncan," he'd say. "I like you. *You* appreciate junk."

Charlie sipped the cocoa and shook his head. He'd done it again: "Who's Molly Pitcher?" he'd asked.

The whole class had groaned.

Charlie had to admit they'd had a lot of practice groaning. His teacher, Mrs. Li, was new. Charlie thought she was neat. Her favorite subject was art, and she had it on Mondays instead of Fridays so they could work on projects all week. "And don't be afraid to ask questions," she said. Charlie had a lot of questions.

"Mrs. Li? Who painted that one?" He pointed at one of the prints that were lined up on the chalkboard. They were samples for a watercolor lesson.

"A man by the name of Winslow Homer."

"Yes, but who *is* he?"

"Good question, Charlie. Try the library for an answer. And, class, I'd like a two-page paper on Winslow Homer. Or any of the painters here." She pointed to each of the prints in turn. "Georgia O'Keeffe, John Singer Sargent, or Edward Hopper. Take your choice."

On another day when they made salt-paste

maps: "Mrs. Li? Look at the way Africa is shaped. It looks like it would fit right there between North and South America."

"Good thinking, Charlie. Geologists saw the same thing. They came up with something called the Plate Tectonics Theory. Try the library to find out about it. And, class, I'd like a three-page report on some aspect of geology. The kinds of rocks we can find around here. Or maybe where most earthquakes occur."

Charlie took a big gulp of cocoa. "Me and my big mouth. I just *had* to ask about Molly Pitcher. But I'll bet Mrs. Li would have assigned those reports on women in the American Revolution anyway," he told a passing spider. "And all the other reports. It's *not* my questions! No matter what Sam says!"

He watched the spider leg it up the six feet of packing-crate wall.

"I can't help it if I always get A's on them. Or that Sam gets F's—when he does them. I bet it wouldn't be so bad if I didn't make us lose so many of our games." At least that's what Sam said. And Sam should know, Charlie thought. He'd been elected captain.

He sipped at the cocoa. Beginning with the

Blue Sox's first game, Sam yelled at Charlie as soon as he put a foot on the field. And with reason, Charlie admitted. Every time he had to work with Sam, he goofed. He'd miss easy passes, fall flat on his face, or let the opposing team walk all over him.

The spider disappeared into a crack.

Spiders never stop to chat, he thought. No one does. Except Mr. Brickle sometimes. And balloons.

Charlie frowned and propped his head up with his hands. "They always tell me great stories about their lives. And then they leave." He thought about Green. "I wonder if they wanted to hear about me like Green did? But I don't do anything interesting."

The spider poked one leg after the other out of the hole. "I'd sure like to see Green," he told the spider. "You should have met him. A real *circus* balloon. Green was great! He knew some of the best stor—"

Charlie stopped mid-word. Did balloons have regular names? They must be called something besides Green or Red or Blue.

"I bet Green is a last name. Like Duncan. I should have asked," he mumbled. As the days and weeks went by, Charlie had wondered and worried about Green. Why had he left so abruptly? Why hadn't he even said good-bye? Maybe Green had more exciting things to do than listen to Charlie read. Maybe . . .

Charlie sucked in air to heave a great sigh, sighed most of it out, but held some back in his cheeks.

He started to rise.

He banged his head on the packing-crate ceiling.

"Hey!" he yelled. And fell back to the floor.

He stared at the ceiling and then at the floor. "It didn't happen," he said. He shook his head. "It couldn't happen." He tried it again.

Inhale. Blow a little out. Fill cheeks.

Up he went!

And banged his head again. But this time he didn't let all the air out at once. Instead, he let it out slowly. And slowly he drifted back to the floor.

A tickle began under his ribs.

"I bet I'm part balloon!" He laughed and tried it again. "Maybe," he said, once his feet were back on the floor, "maybe I'm part balloon the way some people are part Italian."

Charlie finished the hot chocolate, pulled a sheet out of his notebook, and scribbled a thank-you note for Mr. Brickle. He picked up his spelling book and went outside. "Maybe it's like Dad said about Kate the time he found her up in the apple tree—part monkey."

The quickest way out of Mr. Brickle's yard was up and over the packing crate. Then all he had to do was shinny up the old flagpole and drop over the fence. Otherwise he had to back-track through the obstacle course and its mysteries.

Charlie wanted out double-quick. He wanted to tell the whole world he was part balloon. He eyed the flagpole and grinned. Maybe his balloon-ness could help. He inhaled and shot straight off the ground.

Too much lift, he thought as he passed the telephone wires. He let out little puffs of air. Five of them and he was level with the top of the fence.

But it was *there* and he was *here*—three feet away.

Charlie kicked his legs, but nothing happened. He tucked his spelling book under his belt and tried the frog stroke he'd learned at the

Y. Better, he thought. With the help of a passing breeze, he blew toward the fence.

"Hey!" yelled Mr. Brickle. "Are you flying, Charlie Duncan?! You get down from there, you young whippersnapper!"

Charlie looked over his shoulder. Mr. Brickle waved wildly. Charlie nodded vigorously and swam for all he was worth. As soon as he passed the fence, Charlie let his breath out slowly and drifted to the ground.

"I'm down, Mr. Brickle," he called loudly. It sounded like Mr. Brickle was crashing into every obstacle in his yard.

"Were you flying, Charlie Duncan?" he shouted.

"Uh, not exactly, Mr. Brickle. Just, uh, just passing along."

"Well, you be careful, Charlie Duncan. And . . . and stay out of my yard!"

"Yes, sir."

Charlie crunched through the last of the maple leaves. Mr. Brickle had never said *that* before. Not even on his grumpiest days. "Maybe it's because I'm part balloon," he told a bare branch.

He puffed out his cheeks and floated a few feet. Maybe I shouldn't tell anybody, he thought. If Mr. Brickle got so mad, what would somebody like Kate say? Or Sam?

6

One Question Too Many

Mom was home and busy in the kitchen. "Hi, Charlie," she called. "How went your day?"

"Okay," said Charlie. "I thought it was Dad's turn for dinner."

"We traded. What kind of potatoes do you want?"

"Mashed."

"Don't you like other kinds?"

Charlie poked his head into the refrigerator. "Yes, but I like mashed best. There's nothing to eat in here."

Mom laughed. "That refrigerator is full, Charlie."

"I know, but—"

"Try the cookie jar. Dad made peanut butter, and I actually made some chocolate chip."

Charlie took three of each. "Thanks, Mom."

"Where are you going, Charlie?"

"Upstairs. I've got to study."

"Spelling?"

Charlie crossed his eyes and groaned.

"That bad, huh?" said Mom.

Charlie might get A's on his reports, but his spelling grade hovered between C and D. "Homophones. I can never get them straight."

"We called them homonyms when I went to school. As I remember it, I flunked every homonym test I ever took."

"Then you won't be mad if I do?"

"Not very. But it'd be nice if you did better than I."

"Okay, Mom. I'll try. And, Mom?"

"Yes, Charlie?" Mom brushed her hair up off her face with her arm. Flour covered her hands.

How could he tell her he was part balloon? She'd probably haul him off to a doctor. Or at least shove a thermometer in his mouth. He bit into a chocolate-chip cookie. "These are pretty good."

"Thanks for the kind words. I know they're not as good as your father's. But I am getting better, don't you think?"

Charlie nodded and went upstairs. He piled the cookies on his nightstand and flopped on his bed. He propped the spelling book on his pillow. In between bites of cookie, he mumbled spelling words.

"Heard. I heard him yell. H,E,A,R,D. Heard."

People can't be balloons!

"Herd. He had a herd of cattle. H,E,R,D. Herd."

But I did fly!

"Boar. A boar is a mean pig. B,O,A,R. Boar."

I can fly! Just like Green!

"Bore. Spelling is a bore! B,O,R,E. Bore!"

Inhale—and up he went!

The spelling book lay forgotten on the bed. Instead of spelling, he practiced ballooning and frogging around the room. I bet it would be easier if I had a breeze, he thought. He burrowed in the hall closet till he found Mom's electric fan. He was right. It was much easier.

He found out that if he breathed normally through his nose, it didn't affect his lift one way or another. If he puffed more air into his bulging

51

cheeks, he sailed higher. If he let a little air out, he sank. It was easy: Air in—up; air out—down. Soon Charlie learned to regulate how high he went by the amount of air he took in. And once he managed to land back on the bed without wrinkling the bedspread.

He tried talking while aloft but dropped like a stone. That ended that. He'd have to stop before Mom investigated the noise. Charlie knew from experience that three thumps were her limit. If he couldn't talk, he couldn't. And it might be a problem.

Suppose he was way up there and a bird happened by and said "Good afternoon," or whatever the equivalent in Bird would be. The bird would think him impolite if he didn't answer, and if he did—*splat!*

So he practiced smiling and nodding and bowing. It wouldn't be as polite as speaking, but it might get by in a pinch.

At dinner, Charlie kept looking at Mom and Dad and then at Kate. Was Dad part balloon? Mom? Kate? If they were, wouldn't you think they'd have mentioned it? Maybe some other relative was part balloon.

Charlie opened his mouth to ask, but Dad was talking about Saturday's homecoming football game. "I'd like to go," he was saying to Mom, "but Mrs. Goodly wants me to restock her greenhouse. Somebody left the door open and everything died."

"Dad?" Charlie asked before Mom could say anything. "Does anybody in our family—uh, fly?"

Dad paused with the fork halfway to his mouth. "Uncle Harry was in the Air Force."

"Oh."

"Were you thinking of joining up?"

Charlie shook his head. "I just wondered."

"Don't forget Aunt Julie," said Mom. "That crazy little sister of mine has tried parachuting, hang gliding, and gliders."

"I didn't know *that*!" said Kate. "Can I get a hang glider?"

"Not this week," said Mom.

Charlie went back to letting the gravy out of his mashed-potato lake. Aunt Julie. Hmmm. It wasn't quite the same, though.

Maybe it's not like being part Italian. Maybe, he thought, it's an aptitude. Like being good in art or math. Or soccer. Mark seemed to have an aptitude for that. And Kate was good in science. I'll bet that's it, he decided. It's an aptitude.

Charlie had two pieces of apple pie for dessert. It wasn't very good, but Mom tried so hard. She couldn't help it if she didn't have an aptitude for cooking.

The next morning Charlie walked to school with his eyes on the sky. It seemed to stretch forever. He could see himself wheeling and dipping. Flying, soaring! He grinned and took a deep breath and—

"Hey! Charlie! Wait up!"

He jumped. Mark and Joseph were almost on top of him.

Charlie remembered suddenly that he'd wanted Joseph to come over to his house. Mark, too. But ever since that first soccer game, Charlie had kept his mouth shut and tried to be small.

As usual Joseph's hands were shoved deep in his pockets. Mark dribbled his soccer ball. They fell into place beside him and looked at each other.

Uh-oh, thought Charlie. They don't look too happy. He stumbled over a crack.

"Sam called a meeting of the Blue Sox last night," said Joseph.

Charlie made a face. He'd forgotten a meeting! "I'm sorry," he said. "I guess I forgot."

"You weren't invited, Charlie. Sam's mad at you."

Charlie stared at his feet. Was he *that* bad at last week's soccer game? He thought he'd done pretty well. And they had won. "I thought I played okay," he said.

Joseph's hands made fists in his pockets. "It's not that, Charlie. It's that report on those ladies."

Charlie opened his mouth, but Mark cut in. "And we've already done six other reports, Charlie."

"But that's not my fault!"

Joseph and Mark looked at each other again. "You give Mrs. Li the ideas," said Mark.

"Maybe," admitted Charlie. "But my sister says fifth grade is when you start doing lots of reports."

Mark dribbled the ball a couple of feet. Joseph's pockets bulged and flattened. "Sam says he doesn't want to do any more reports," Joseph said finally.

Charlie hunted around for something to say. "Sam doesn't do many of the reports anyway," he tried.

Mark nodded. "He's tired of getting into trouble."

"Anyway, Charlie, we thought you ought to know." Joseph took his hands out of his pockets. This must be important, Charlie thought. Joseph never waved his hands around unless it was. "We don't like secret meetings and we don't like threats."

"Sam thinks he's king, not captain," Mark put in.

"Right," said Joseph. "But, uh . . ."

"But I shouldn't ask any more questions?"

They nodded.

"I don't do it on purpose, you know."

They nodded again. Joseph's hands disappeared.

"I'll try," said Charlie.

The day limped along. Mostly Charlie stared out the window. He wished he were out there— up there. Mrs. Li gave the weekly spelling test right after lunch. They traded papers and corrected them. When Charlie got his paper back, he stared at all the red marks. He'd missed ten out of seventeen. Not even Sam had done that badly. He knew; he'd corrected Sam's paper. Maybe he should have studied spelling instead of lift.

He shrugged the thought away and stared out the window again. If you're good at something, he thought, you should use it. But how could he use his balloon-ness?

Kites got all tangled in high wires. He could untangle them. Or he could rescue cats from trees. Or—*wow!*—he could rescue people from burning buildings. He'd be a hero!

Dumb! he thought, and slumped down in his chair. Unless the person was pretty small, how could he carry anyone? And nobody flew kites in November. It'd be months before the kites came out. And all the cats he knew climbed up and down trees with no trouble at all. He slumped farther down.

"What can I do?" he muttered. He chewed on a piece of his spelling test.

"Did you have a question, Charlie?" asked Mrs. Li.

Charlie shook his head as the class groaned. He didn't even know what they were doing. One quick glance told him English. He yanked out his language book and opened it, then stared at a page without seeing any of the words.

If he'd known he was part balloon when Green was visiting, they could have gone places together. If he'd known, maybe Green would have stayed longer.

Not forever though, he decided. After all, Green was a balloon, and Charlie was mostly boy. As much as he liked Green, if he was honest with himself, he knew he wouldn't mind having some people friends. He snuck a look at Joseph and Mark. They'd make good friends. It was nice of them to warn him. Maybe if he weren't so rotten on the soccer field and if he stopped asking dumb questions, they'd like to come to dinner or something.

Balloons must feel the same way. He saw them at fairs and circuses. Hundreds—all their strings tied together at one point.

If he went looking for Green, he'd have to find a group like that to help him.

"Mrs. Li?" he asked without thinking.

"What's a group of balloons called? You know, like a covey of quail or a swarm of bees?"

There was a low growl of gasps, and Sam said quickly, "A bunch of balloons."

"How about a flock?" Joseph chimed in.

"I know," said Mark, with a glance at Charlie. "A school of balloons."

"A herd?" asked Girard.

"No," said Joseph with a grin. "That's a herd of turtles!"

"Enough," said Mrs. Li. "But it's an interesting idea. Think about it over the weekend and come in Monday with your best guesses."

One loud groan came from twenty-seven throats.

"For pity's sake!" snapped Mrs. Li. She slammed her language book on the desk. "I'm not asking for a report! Only a *word*. And you needn't even write it down!"

Charlie closed his eyes against the black looks and Sam's curling lip. He knew it didn't matter what Mrs. Li assigned—a report or a single word. He'd done it again!

7

One Answer Too Many

When the final bell rang, Sam led the Friday stampede through the door.

"Charlie!" Mrs. Li raised her voice over the clatter. "Will you stay a minute?"

Charlie dragged himself up to her desk. No one had even looked at him all afternoon. Except Sam—he'd caught Charlie's eye once or twice and curled his lip. That was worse.

Mrs. Li tapped her knuckle on the Halloween bulletin board by her desk. "This has *got* to come down. I'm getting dark looks from the principal." She pulled pins out of witches and bats.

Charlie had the creepy feeling that somewhere someone was pushing pins into a picture of him.

"Anyway, I wanted to thank you, Charlie." He looked blank. "For giving me another idea for this bulletin board. It'll be a lot more colorful and much less work. The class will never know you saved them from writing a couple of pages about adjectives."

Charlie tried to smile, but he felt sick.

"Is something wrong, Charlie?"

"Uh, could you tell everybody? About the board? And the extra work and all that?"

Mrs. Li nodded. "It *was* a pretty loud groan, wasn't it?"

"Yeah," said Charlie. He doubted that Mrs. Li's telling them would help much. They *never* had homework on Fridays, and even if it was only one lousy little word, it was still homework. It was the wedge that would open the door to weekend reports. He knew it and so did everybody else.

He shifted his soccer shoes from one shoulder to the other and inched away. "I've got soccer practice," he mumbled.

"Have a good weekend, Charlie."

Everyone was on the field when Charlie arrived. Coach Tyler ran along the far side, yelling for accuracy. "Think before you kick!" he shouted. *"Think!"*

As usual, Charlie had worn a pair of shorts under his jeans. He sat on the grass to change his shoes and watched Sam jump to deflect a pass. He missed.

"Not high enough," Charlie told his socks. A glimmering of an idea twitched through his mind. "Not high enough. Hmmm. Not enough lift! I've got it!" Charlie jumped up. Here was a place he could use his balloon-ness!

Mrs. Coach, Coach Tyler's wife and the assistant coach, trotted over to Charlie. "What are you doing here, Charlie? You should be home in bed."

Charlie stared at her. What was she talking about?

"It's all right, Charlie. The boys told me about your sore throat. Missing one practice won't hurt. Even missing tomorrow's game. Don't worry, we'll win even without our best sweeper." She clucked like mothers do. "You look pale, Charlie." She reached out to feel his forehead.

Charlie flinched away. *The* boys *told me* . . .

"You should get right home and into bed. We want you healthy for next Wednesday's game. You know it'll be the toughest one of the season."

Charlie opened his mouth. He closed it again. He couldn't think of anything to say. *The* boys *told me* . . . Slowly he reached down for his jeans.

"Don't forget the note from your mother, Charlie."

What note? he wondered, and looked up.

"The note about your sore throat," said Mrs. Coach. "League rules. You have to be healthy to play, you know."

Charlie barely heard her. He stared over her shoulder.

Sam stood there. Smiling.

So that's it, Charlie thought, and crammed on a running shoe.

"Charlie?" said Mrs. Coach. "You don't look well. Shall I drive you home?"

"No," Charlie got out. His voice was hoarse.

"You don't sound too good either, Charlie," said Sam in a phony voice. "If you get *really* sick, maybe your mommy will buy you a balloon."

"Nonsense!" said Mrs. Coach. "Charlie's too old for balloons."

Sam grinned nastily. "Oh, I don't know about that."

"Sam!" hollered Coach Tyler. "Get out here!"

"See you, Charlie." Sam took a step toward him. "Hope you feel better . . ." he lowered his voice ". . . in about a year!"

"Sam!"

"Coming!"

"Sure I can't drive you home, Charlie?"

Charlie just shook his head. As he walked away, Coach was still yelling, *"Think!"* Charlie put one foot in front of the other. He couldn't see very well, but he wasn't crying. He wasn't!

Sam wanted him off the team. *The* boys *told me . . . They* wanted him off the team! Over a stupid homework assignment! This was their answer to his question about balloons. He thought Joseph and Mark kind of liked him. After all, they'd warned him. Warned him. *The* boys *told me . . .*

"I won't think about it!" he yelled at a maple tree. "I won't! I'll think about something else. I'll think about Green. *He* likes me!"

Charlie's voice was shaky. He kicked at a

rock. "And I can ask him what a group of balloons is called. He's sure to know." He kicked at another rock. "I'll have the best answer in class."

"Talking to yourself again, Charlie Duncan?" Mr. Brickle was leaning against the door of his shop.

Charlie gulped and nodded.

"Maybe if you thought a bit before you opened your mouth, you'd have somebody to talk to instead of rocks and trees and such, Charlie Duncan."

"Maybe," said Charlie.

"You ought to let a thought rattle around in your head for a bit before you let it out, Charlie Duncan. Plan a little. What's the assignment this time?"

Charlie had told Mr. Brickle about all the questions he asked at the wrong time. "Only a word, Mr. Brickle."

"What word?"

"What a group of balloons is called."

Mr. Brickle raised his bushy eyebrows. "Balloons, huh?" He nodded to himself and pushed himself away from the doorjamb. "About yesterday."

Uh-oh, Charlie thought. Here it comes.

"I think I was a mite hasty. You're welcome in my yard, Charlie Duncan."

"Thanks, Mr. Brickle."

"Balloons," Mr. Brickle repeated in a low voice. "Could be," he muttered. He nodded again and disappeared into his shop.

Charlie stared after him. That's weird, he thought. Nothing about my flying. But then, Mr. Brickle never said or did anything Charlie expected. He dribbled a medium-sized rock down the street with his feet. There were bigger things to worry about than Mr. Brickle.

To find Green, he'd have to have a plan.

"I'll take some money," he told a holly bush. "When I get hungry, I can land and buy a hot dog. After all, it might take days to find Green."

Charlie stared at the bush as though it had said something. "I am *not* running away!" he shouted at it. "Not exactly, anyway," he said turning away. "I'm just going to visit Green. And maybe he'll ask me to stay for a while. It wouldn't be polite to rush off. Mom says so."

He started running. He'd think about that later. When he could think about everybody lying and nobody liking him. After he found

Green. That's when he'd think about all that stuff. After he found Green.

He tripped over a root. He lay there, getting his breath back and calling himself names. "Dummy!" he said, picking himself up and wiping his eyes. He *wasn't* crying! He must have hit his nose on that dumb root. Fifth graders never cried. He swallowed hard and walked on.

"Where do I start looking for Green?" he asked himself. He couldn't fly off in all directions at once. If he went north, the balloon might be south. If he went west, Green might be east—or south, or anywhere. He kicked another rock a couple of feet. "Other balloons would know. But where can I find one to ask?" The circus and the fair had come and gone for the year. Where could he find balloons?

He scratched his nose and looked around as though he expected a balloon to pop out from behind a bush. None did.

"Think," said Coach. "Think," said Mr. Brickle.

Charlie leaned against a tree. "Think," he told himself. "Where do you see balloons?" Something nudged the edge of his mind. Something Dad had said at dinner. Charlie hadn't really been listening. What was it?

Something about a football game.

Football. Halftime. Bands. Balloons!

That was it! At all the halftimes Charlie had seen on television, they'd let out millions of balloons! He nodded. He'd be at the stadium Saturday afternoon and see who he could find.

8

Brunhilda

Charlie was up early Saturday as usual, but he watched the sunrise from his window rather than the porch. The sky was red, and it looked cold out there! There was frost on the window-pane and on the grass. He shivered. What if that weatherman was right? A slight chance of snow, he'd said. He'd have to wear those dumb long johns or he'd freeze.

Charlie did all his Saturday chores and then raced upstairs to change. He felt like an over-stuffed polar bear as he tucked his flap cap under his belt. Ordinarily he wouldn't be caught dead wearing a flap cap, but his ears got very cold very fast. He could always hide the flaps inside the cap. His mittens went into his back pockets.

He raided his hedgehog bank and stuffed all the dimes, nickels, and quarters into his pants pockets. They bulged. He took a deep breath and puffed out his cheeks.

His heels lifted from the floor, but his toes didn't. He'd have to trade for dollar bills. Mom and Dad were both at work. He couldn't ask them anyway; they'd ask why he wasn't in his soccer uniform.

Charlie poked his head around Kate's door. She was lying on her back, her legs stretched up the wall. Weird, he thought. But now would not be the time to say anything. "Kate? Will you trade dollars for coins?"

Kate tilted her head back to look at him. "What for?"

"The coins make my pockets bulge." Well, they do, he told himself. "I look like a sideways kangaroo."

"Okay. The money's in the bottom drawer."

Charlie pulled his coins out and made stacks.

71

"One, two, three, four. And seventy-five cents."

"Why are you dressed for the North Pole? I thought you had a game today."

Charlie's stomach jumped. "Uh, not today." He dumped the change into Kate's drawer and stuffed the four dollars into his jacket pocket with the seventy-five cents. "See you, Kate. Thanks."

By the time Charlie turned into the park path that led to the football stadium, he was hot and sticky and irritable. The long johns itched like crazy, his snow jacket felt like an electric blanket, and where was the stupid snow? There wasn't a cloud in the sky!

Charlie walked around until he found a spot where the cheers from the stadium were loudest. He knew that if sounds blew toward him, the balloons would come this way too. He sat down under a tree to wait; but when he heard the signal ending the first half, he couldn't sit still any longer.

He inhaled and floated himself to the top of the tree. The wind was stronger there. And colder. He held on to a twig with his feet and pulled on his flap cap. The mittens would have to wait. He couldn't grab a string with mittened hands.

Charlie waited forever. At least it felt that way. There was time to think of millions of questions. What if there aren't any balloons? he worried. What if someone sees me? What if . . . ?

There they came! Hundreds of them! Thousands! Scarlet and gold, sky-blue and yellow.

Charlie let go of the tree. Up he went!

All at once he was surrounded by talking, laughing, giggling balloons.

"Lovely day, isn't it?" said one.

"I thought we'd never get out of that smelly box!" exclaimed another. "Great wind lift though."

"How high the sky is today!" said an elongated Red.

"How *blue*," corrected a round blue one.

Several said, "Good afternoon, young man." They all sniffed and turned away when he only nodded back.

Smiling (which was *very* difficult with his cheeks puffed out) and nodding, Charlie grabbed for string after string. But either the balloons themselves were avoiding him or the wind was dancing them just out of his reach.

At last he got his fingers around the string of a big fat yellow one. She didn't like it and started yelling.

"Young man! I say, *young man!* Let me go! How *dare* you!"

Charlie tried to smile wider and to nod and to search for a likely-looking landing place all at the same time.

The balloon kept yelling.

Charlie and the yellow balloon drifted beyond the town limits before he spotted a meadow with a few leftover wildflowers. Firs and hemlock marched in a semicircle around its edge, but they were far enough away not to be a danger. He closed one eye to judge the center of the meadow.

To hit it, he let out the last of his air while he was still about four feet up. He landed with a jolt, and the yellow balloon seemed to go pale lemon.

"Young man! This is *too much!* Let me *go!*"

"Yes, ma'am. In a minute, ma'am." Charlie sat on a rock and tried to get his breath back. "I hope I didn't scare you."

"*Scare me?* What would you think if some

upstart with woolly ears grabbed *you* and sank *you* to earth?"

"My ears aren't woolly," Charlie said, lifting the flaps. "It's a cap. I'm sorry if I scared you, but I just have to talk with a balloon."

"Humph!" she snorted. "I don't speak with *strangers*."

"Oh," said Charlie. This wasn't according to his plan. Who would have thought he'd catch a grouchy balloon? He scratched his nose and tried to think.

Mr. Brickle said to plan out what you were going to say, but what could you say to an angry balloon? He remembered something Mom said about being polite to old ladies even when they're not polite to you. Maybe it would work with a grouchy balloon.

"I know I've interrupted your journey, ma'am," he said in his politest voice. "But I need some information. I thought you could help me."

"Well-l-l-l, I do know *most* everything." She swayed in the breeze and spun slowly so that the sun glinted on her fat sides. "Not to *brag,* but I *am* one of the *better* balloons. *Very* well educated. Though my *dear* Papa was not *quite* sure about the *necessity* for *all* that knowledge."

Charlie nodded and nodded. Not even Kate talked with so many italics.

"At *least* you're a *mannerly* boy. I'll give you *that*. What is it you need to know?"

"Yes, ma'am. Thank you, ma'am." His mind went blank. All those words! He never had trouble with questions in school. Not *asking* them anyway. Why couldn't he think? "Do you have a name?" he asked at last. "I mean, do balloons have names?"

"*Young man! You* certainly haven't been well educated. *Of course* we have names! Do you think we are *pumpkins*?" Her voice dropped a full octave. "I am Brunhilda—of the *Sun* Yellow branch of the family. And I'll have you know that *many* of my ancestors were of the *Gold*!" She snorted again. "Humph!"

"Yes, ma'am—Brunhilda. Sorry, ma'am."

"If *that's* all . . ."

"No, ma'am," Charlie said. "I'm looking for a friend."

"What's her name?"

"He's a him, ma'am. And that's the trouble. I don't know his name."

"If *you* don't know his name, how do you expect *me* to help?"

"I thought you could tell me where the balloons who visit boys go when the visit is up."

"*Good gracious!* If they should *survive* such a *ghastly* experience—which is *doubtful*—they may go to one of several places. It depends upon their *point of origin.*"

"I met my friend at the circus that came through here last August."

"The *circus*? We *never* have *anything* to do with *that* branch of the family." She bounced around and managed to look insulted.

"Be polite, be polite," Charlie muttered under his breath. "You're so well educated, I was sure you'd know." Charlie rolled his eyes.

"Well-l-l-l . . ." She swayed in the breeze. "I *might.*"

Charlie's heart jumped.

"You'll have to *promise* not to tell," she whispered.

"Cross my heart."

Brunhilda bumped about and started to say something three times before she blurted, "My brother Digby is the black balloon of the family. We *never* speak of him. He left to join the circus. In Peoria. I did some checking, and . . ." She looked around as though to make sure no one was listening. "You *do* promise, don't you?"

Charlie nodded and solemnly crossed his heart. Digby must be with Green!

"I got a message from him," she whispered. "A passing blimp delivered it. Cousins, you know. *Distant* cousins."

"That's great! Nice for you, I mean."

Brunhilda nodded and sighed. "He was my favorite brother." She drooped, and sniffed back a tear.

Charlie shook his head. Who would have thought that anyone so conceited would love someone so very ordinary as a balloon who wanted to join the circus. It just showed that the outside of a balloon isn't all there is. Poor Brunhilda, Charlie thought. "Maybe you could visit him sometime," he said, hoping she wouldn't want to go with him. "Where is he?"

"Florida."

"Florida!" Charlie yelped. "You mean the *state* Florida?"

"Young man, what *other* Florida is there?"

Charlie's stomach hit the ground. Florida was

two thousand miles away. "Florida," he repeated dully. "It'll take days to get there."

Brunhilda gave him a look. "May I *go* now?" she snapped huffily.

Charlie gulped. He knew that look; Kate looked at him just like that. "Yes, ma'am," he said. "But are you sure that's where all the balloons go?"

"I don't *recall* that I said *all* balloons went there. You asked me where *Digby* went."

"Yes, ma'am. Would Green—that's what I call him—have gone there, too?"

"Tch, tch, tch. 'Green.' *Surely* you must have a better description than 'green.' What *color* green? Lime? Grass? Apple? Leaf? Olive? Nile?"

Charlie closed his eyes to shut out all the words. "He's the color of a ring my mother has. Lightish."

"You mean jade?"

"That's what she calls it! Do you know him?"

"*Not* personally, but I know his branch of the family: the Jade Greens. We have *very little* in common and seldom meet. I heard they didn't join *the* circus—Ringling, you know—but travel with a *small* one. Jupiter's Splendiferous Super

Stupendous, I think. They winter in Weston Town."

"Brunhilda! That's the one!" Charlie wanted to hug her. Weston Town was only twenty miles away! He could fly there in no time.

Brunhilda's voice dropped as though she were telling something awful. "I've heard that they ship their elephants to California for the winter. Cold, you know. Elephants are so *susceptible* to colds." She paused and glanced around. "They can't afford a *proper* wagon for them," she whispered.

Charlie squirmed. He tried to remember that she loved her black sheep—uh, balloon brother, Digby. But it was hard. Charlie liked Jupiter's Splendiferous Super Stupendous Circus. It was just the right size for him. He decided he and Brunhilda should part company. He stood up.

"Thank you very much, Brunhilda ma'am. Would you like to be let go here? Or up there?" He pointed toward the sky.

Brunhilda looked around. "There don't *appear* to be any thornbushes. I believe I can get a *proper* lift from here."

Charlie let go of the string. "Thanks again, ma'am," he called. He sat down. As much as he

81

wanted to find Green, he wanted to wait until Brunhilda got a big head start. Even though she'd been a great help, he didn't want to have to talk with her anytime soon. All that ma'am-ing!

Brunhilda rose higher and higher. She cleared the advancing hemlocks with a good six feet to spare and never looked back.

Charlie rested his chin on his hand. She hadn't even bothered to ask what he'd been doing up there in the sky. "She could have asked," he told a grasshopper. "I would have. I mean, you don't meet part-balloon boys every day. And she never asked my name," he added grumpily. "For someone who knows most everything, she sure doesn't seem to know how to be polite. Even if she does love her ordinary brother."

Charlie looked toward the trees. There wasn't a glimmer of yellow.

"Not even Kate is that conceited!" Before he pulled on his mittens, he checked the wind direction. Just right. He covered his ears.

"Weston Town!" he shouted. "Here I come!" He took a very deep breath and puffed out his cheeks.

But instead of going straight up, the wind caught him as his feet left the ground. It hurled him toward the line of trees. Charlie pumped more air into his cheeks until he couldn't puff one more puff without losing it all.

The hemlocks and firs were getting closer and bigger.

This is it, he told himself. He closed his eyes and tucked up his feet.

9

A Rough Ride ...

An updraft caught him.

His feet scraped a tree crown, but he made it. Charlie almost sighed in relief, but remembered where he was.

Up he went. Higher and higher, swept along by the wind. He relaxed. After all, he thought, there isn't much you can run into up here. He puffed out a little air and let himself glide.

The world below looked like a map. All neat angles and squared-off fields. The farmhouses and barns could be part of his train set; the animals fit into his miniature Noah's Ark.

From up here everything seemed new and clean, a part of everything else. Hills and lakes, rivers and roads, trees, fields, land and sky— they all merged into a glorious whole.

For the moment Charlie's problems seemed smaller than the late lambs huddling by their mothers. What did it matter that Sam was an idiot, when he'd been blessed with this gift of flight? A glow spread through him. To be part of all this! He promised himself he'd never forget that—if only for a little while—he'd recognized and been part of the magic of the universe.

A trill of notes sounded in his ear. He jerked, gasped, and dropped a few feet.

It was a lark!

He *knew* he was going to run into a bird.

The lark adjusted her glide and flew down till she was on a level with Charlie's eyes. She trilled again.

Charlie shook his head and hunched his shoulders. She ignored that and sang what sounded to be the same notes.

He groaned. The whole bird family will think I'm rude!

Hey! he thought. If I can groan, I can hum! He

hummed some random notes, but the lark looked puzzled and chirped questioningly. Maybe I can hum a message, he thought.

Making up a tune to go with the words, Charlie carefully thought out, "Good afternoon, good afternoon, lovely lark. It's a wonderful day for flying, is it not?"

"Thank you, young sir, for your compliment. It is a day to fill with joy. But you seem to be a boy, not a bird. What are you doing up here?"

Charlie understood Lark! He was so excited, he wanted to shout and sing, but he controlled himself and hummed, "I am a boy who is part balloon, and I'm on my way to Weston Town." He almost thought "Toon" to rhyme with "balloon" but caught himself in time. "I'm visiting a friend," he added.

"It's been long and long since one of you flew with me. And *he* wasn't a boy, but grown already into a man."

"Another flyer?" hummed Charlie excitedly. "Who?"

The lark chirped the equivalent of a shrug. "He could not sing a note. I am most pleased that you can sing. You have a lovely hum."

"I thank you for the thought, my friend. I

haven't had much practice. But I believe, I do indeed, that *you* have a golden, flowing voice. A song to fill the sky."

The lark sang some high notes Charlie didn't understand. She dipped her wings and did a double somersault. She climbed straight up and sleeked back her wings to dive straight down. She pulled up a foot in front of Charlie's nose. "You are an unusual boy!" she trilled.

"My!" Charlie hummed. "You sure can fly!"

"Try!" she sang.

Charlie flung out his arms.

Suddenly, he was tumbling, heels over head. By the time he slowed his rolling, he was facing the way he'd come. He glanced down.

The land was whipping by! Chatting with the lark, Charlie hadn't noticed how fast he was being herded through the sky. He looked up. His heart hit his toes.

Boiling up behind him were billowing, frothing thunderheads. Lashed by the wind, they spilled blacks and grays across the arc of blue. The sun stained their edges with angry reds and purples. "Uh-oh," Charlie hummed as he turned himself around. "I think that we're in trouble."

"You should find your nest, young sir. These

twisting clouds are danger filled; even trees will shake." She hesitated. "You are too big to share my nest, else you could hide with me."

"It's kind of you to think of me, but go I must to Weston Town. Is this wild wind still blowing there?"

"If you mean the town that has a statue of a general,"—Charlie nodded—"then, large friend, this wildness will, in anger, blow you townward." She gathered her wings for her dive. "Fly safely!"

"Wait!" Charlie hummed. "I would like to ask your name. Mine is Charlie Duncan."

"Lovely!" caroled the lark. "And I am called Sapphira." Her notes ran almost too high to hear. "It means beautiful."

"You are beautiful, Sapphira! A safe journey home." Charlie wanted to wave but was afraid of rolling again.

"Good-bye, Charlie Duncan!"

Charlie watched Sapphira fly out of sight. He'd never thought much of his name before. It was just a name. But Sapphira had transformed it, made it—magical.

And someone else had flown with Sapphira.

Who could it have been? Did Sapphira mean someone like him, someone part balloon? Or someone like Aunt Julie, who tootled around the sky on a hang glider? I wonder, he thought, if Green ever met somebody like me? I'll ask him.

He glanced over his shoulder. The clouds were nearly on him. And suddenly, it was colder—much colder. He zipped his jacket and turned up the collar. There was still a long way to go.

Something slammed into his back. He was spinning. Tumbling. Wheeling. Falling.

Charlie flung out his arms and legs and pushed against the air. It took a lot of tries, but he finally stopped rolling. He was still dizzy and cross-eyed when everything went fuzzy. The storm had caught him.

He shot straight up—and dropped straight down. Up! Down! Up! Air pockets bounced him around like a pinball.

Water ran off his jacket and dripped from his nose.

It's worse than a roller coaster in here, he thought. He had to get out. He blew air out in tiny puffs until the clouds were above him.

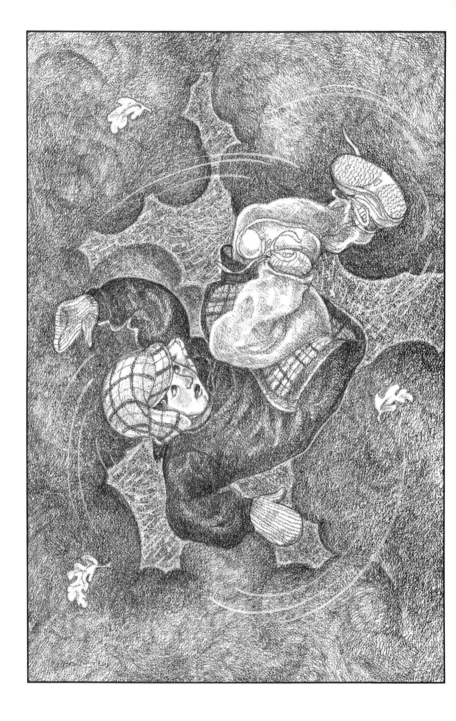

Large, crisp snowflakes hit him in the face. What do you know? he thought. The weather-man was right.

His nose began to run. He kept wiping at it with his mitten. Tears from the cold ran down his face. His cheeks were so cold, they were numb. How could he keep them puffed out?

It got harder to breathe. If only my nose would stop running! he thought frantically. But still the wind drove him onward.

He could barely see. What if he ran into a tree or a chimney? He was still too high to let go of all the air. What if . . . ?

He sneezed.

10

... And a Rougher Landing

Falling!

He was falling! If he hit at this speed—*splat!*

Charlie snatched a breath and puffed out his cheeks. He slowed down a little. Enough? He hoped so.

He was almost not afraid anymore when—*wham!*—he slammed into something. Something cold and wet and hard.

Breathing in big deep gulps of air and listening to his heart pound, he just lay there being glad he was lying there breathing and listening. After a long time, he blinked and looked around.

Where was he? The ground was a long way down.

His arms were wrapped around a horse's neck. One foot rested on a sword; the other was jammed into a brass belt buckle.

The statue of the general! He'd made it to Weston Town.

"I never kicked a general in the stomach before," he said as he climbed down. He rubbed his chest and stood there grinning up at the unsmiling general. "It feels more like you kicked me, but thanks for the save."

Even as Charlie stood there watching, the snow piled up on the general's hat. He shivered. Snow was piling up on him, too. He ran across the park and ducked into a dark doorway. The general gradually disappeared. Snow was being driven almost parallel to the ground. That was no nice little breeze out there. He'd have to walk the rest of the way.

But the rest of the way where? he wondered. Where do circuses hole up for the winter? They wouldn't be in the middle of a town. They'd need space for all those wagons, even if they did ship their elephants west for the winter. Jupiter's

Splendiferous Super Stupendous Circus would have to be on the edge of town.

"But a town has a lot of edges," he muttered. Those last couple of miles had been a wild ride. His eyes and nose streaming, water dripping from his flap cap. But had he seen *anything* that would or could give him a clue?

Streetlights had popped on. Business lights. House lights. And farther out, strings of Christmas lights.

"No one puts Christmas lights up this early!" he said, watching the little puffs his breath made. "Not before Thanksgiving. But circuses do!" At least, Jupiter's Splendiferous Super Stupendous Circus had last August.

Charlie jammed his hands into his pockets and stepped into the swirling snow. Lumpy shapes hurried by him. Home to dinner? he wondered. His stomach growled, but he told it to shut up and kept walking. He'd have to worry about eating later.

One by one the lumps disappeared up walks. The wind swooped in circles, and Charlie fought for every step. Even with the snow at his back, it was hard to see.

"This running-away business isn't all it's cracked up to be," he sputtered as a tree dumped its load of snow on him.

. . . running-away business . . . running away . . . running . . .

The words thumped and bumped.

Running away?

Charlie stopped and let the wind whip around him. He wasn't visiting Green. He was running away.

"Only cowards run away!" the wind shrieked.

"I'm not a coward!" he yelled, and fought his way forward.

"Chicken!"

"No!" Charlie yelled.

The wind howled and pushed him back. "Old Runaway Charlie. Can't stand up for himself!"

"They don't want me on the team!"

The wind snickered. "You should have stood up to Sam."

"He'll kill me!"

"See! Chicken!"

"That's not true!" Charlie shouted.

He stumbled over a boundary marker. Right in front of him, nestled together like a wagon train in the old west, were the yellow and green wagons of Jupiter's Splendiferous Super Stupendous Circus. Christmas lights strung on and between the wagons glowed mistily through the snow.

Charlie just stood there. Maybe I should go home, he thought. What if Green doesn't remember me?

Charlie shrugged. Or shivered. He wasn't sure which. "I've come this far," he muttered, sliding down a snowbank. "I can't run away all the time."

Luckily no one was outside in this storm, but light leaked out of several shutters. He decided not to try those unless he had to.

Most people wouldn't think to give balloons a light to read by. Green had spent one whole morning trying to figure out how to get some picture books into his circus wagon. "Usually the only things around our place," he'd said, "are old newspapers and maybe a playbill or two. My family would *love* this one." He'd tapped his string on *The Red Balloon*. "I don't mind telling you, kid, it made me cry. Made me proud, it did. Real proud."

Charlie snuck up to a pitch-black wagon. He

inhaled a little, rose up, and knocked. Then he set himself back down and called out very quietly, "Green!"

No answer. He kept trying. At the fourth wagon, the shutter suddenly opened. A gruff voice called out, "Who's that? What do you want?"

"I'm looking for a balloon of the Jade Green family."

As soon as the words were out of his mouth, he groaned. Dummy! he yelled at himself. What if it's a *human* person? Why don't you ever *think?*

But for once it was all right.

"There are some Jade Greens in here. Who do you want?"

"I don't know his name," Charlie apologized. His stomach played funny tricks, as though it had its own air pockets. "He stayed with me for a while. In August."

"Are you a balloon?" the voice asked suspiciously.

"No, sir. Only part balloon. The rest is boy."

"*Boy!* What do you mean coming here in the middle— well, beginning, of winter and disturbing decent balloons? Go away!"

The shutter slammed shut.

11

Green at Last

"Wait!" Charlie yelped. He inhaled and shot up to the shutter.

"Well, I'll be blowed!" A great round jade-green balloon stared out at him. "You *are* part balloon! Come in! Come in, I say. It's snowing!"

It was very dark inside the wagon. The only light seeped in through cracks. Balloons of various colors and in various states of blown–up-ness lounged about the walls and ceiling. Some were long and skinny; some were short and thin; some were shaped like pears; a few were round as beach balls.

"Now, then," yawned the balloon who let him in. "What can I do for you?"

"I'm sorry to bother you, but I was looking—"

"I know you!" said a voice above his head. "You're that kid who plays soccer and knows great stories."

It was Green!

"How ya been, kid?"

Charlie was so excited, he shot straight up to the ceiling. He opened his mouth to say "Fine," and hit the floor with a thump. "Forgot," he mumbled. "Could you come down here to talk?"

"If you give me a hand," said Green. "No breeze in here."

Charlie wrapped the string around his mitten and pulled. He'd found Green! He rested his back against the wall and sighed. He remembers me, he thought thankfully.

The balloon who had let Charlie in dangled in a corner and began to snore loudly.

"Never thought you'd visit me, kid!" Green bobbed up and down. "I'm glad to see you! Glad you dropped in. But if you'd been much later, you wouldn't have found anyone up."

"Were you going to bed? Is it *that* late?" If it was, Dad would kill him. If Mom didn't get him first.

But I'm running away. Aren't I? he asked himself.

"Season-late, kid," Green said. "Time for a long sleep. Not much going on for balloons in winter. We're like bears. We hibernate.

"All the other families have been asleep for a month or more. Jade Greens are talkers though. Somebody always knows 'just one more' story. Hugo over there," Green nodded at the snoring balloon, "just told one of the scariest ghost stories I ever heard. Turned a Kelly Green pale yellow."

"Oh," said Charlie. How could he say what he wanted to say? Somebody had told him you begin at the beginning and go on from there. He gulped and said, "I'm sorry if I was rude."

"Rude?"

"I never asked your name."

Green hesitated. "I didn't ask yours either. Somehow I never thought of it. You were just 'kid.' "

"The same with me," Charlie said. "I always thought of you as Green, and then I found out I was part balloon, and—"

"Part balloon! I *knew* you were a good kid!" exclaimed Green. "When I saw you coming down the midway, I just *knew* there was something special about you!"

Something special about me? thought Charlie. "Anyway," he said, "I'm Charles David Duncan. Everybody calls me Charlie."

"My name is Nathaniel," said the balloon. "Nathaniel Jade Green. People call me Windy, but I don't like it much."

Charlie could understand that. "I'll call you Nathaniel," said Charlie. "Or Nat. Or Nate. Which do you like best?"

The balloon thought a minute. "Nathaniel. No one ever calls me Nathaniel. I like the sound of it. Nathaniel." He made each syllable separate and seemed to swell a little. "Say, kid— uh, Charlie. How'd you find me?"

"I met a Sun Yellow named Brunhilda. . . ."

"Brunhilda? She actually *talked* to you? Of all the Sun Yellows, she's the *worst!* And most of the rest of them don't think we're entitled to air space.

"Except her brother Digby. Met him once. Seemed to have his head in the clouds. An all-around good balloon. Why, on the day we met, there was this squirt with a pin, and . . ."

As Green's story rambled on, Charlie began to

relax. It was quiet here in the dark with only Green's voice droning in his ear. This was the first time in a long time he'd been able just to sit quietly. He felt like he'd been running flat out just to keep up with himself. Quiet . . . Dark . . . Quiet . . . Charlie sagged and shook himself awake. "Nathaniel?"

"Huh?"

"Did you ever meet any other part-balloon people?"

Nathaniel thought for almost a full minute. "No. Can't say I remember any, and I'd think I would. And somebody would have mentioned— Hey! Wait!

"Hey, Hugo! Wake up!"

"Hummpft?" muttered Hugo.

"Do you remember that story Great-uncle Peter used to tell? The one about that guy he met?"

Hugo yawned. "You mean the guy he met over the big top in Waterbury?"

"That's the one! What happened?"

"Don't remember . . ." Hugo's voice trailed off into a snore.

"Sorry, kid. When he wakes up, I'll ask him."

"Okay," said Charlie. "Can we get together

later? In spring, maybe? You'll be bored again, but maybe now that I'm part balloon, it won't be so bad."

"What do you mean, kid? I wasn't bored."

"You weren't? I couldn't understand why you just disappeared that day. The only thing I could think of was that you must have been bored stiff by all the reading."

"And I thought you were just being polite, listening to my little tales. After all, there you were with your team. I could tell you and your friends were—well, close. You had to be, to work together like that. Of course, there was that twerp. But I figured that between you and all your friends, you could take care of him. And I could see that you wouldn't have much time left over for me. Wouldn't be right to take you away from your friends."

Friends! Charlie's mouth went dry.

"Balloons get around a lot," Nathaniel went on when Charlie didn't say anything, "but I hardly ever get to talk with somebody interesting. Not somebody like you, Charlie—a soccer player with a lot of friends." He paused. "Hey! Now that you're part balloon, you should be able to get the highest passes."

Charlie swallowed hard. "I thought of that," he mumbled. "But— well, uh, I'm not sure I'm still on the team and . . ." His voice petered out. "Will you tell me something?"

"Sure, Charlie."

Charlie licked his lips. "What would you do if someone lied about you?"

"Punch him in the nose," Nathaniel said promptly. "Of course, I couldn't really. No hands. But I'd think of something. But I can't think of anything worse than being lied about. Except maybe *being* a liar."

"Would you run away?"

Nathaniel took a long time to answer. "I don't know, kid. Would you?"

"Well, I thought I might. But it seems kind of chicken."

"Seems that way to me too, Charlie. And besides, you'd never do anything like that. You're too *special*!"

Charlie stared at the balloon. That's the second time he's said I'm special, thought Charlie. Me. Charlie Duncan. "You're special too, Nathaniel," he said. "Thanks."

Do balloons blush? Charlie wondered. There was a distinct rosy glow to Nathaniel. But maybe it was the Christmas lights. There were a lot of red ones.

"You're a good friend, Charlie. Chasing way out here. With the snow and all." The balloon cleared his throat a couple of times.

Charlie smiled. He knew how Nathaniel felt. He hated it when anyone caught him doing something nice. Maybe Mr. Brickle did too. Maybe that's why he'd never accept Charlie's thanks.

"And I really liked your books," Nathaniel said in a different voice. "You have some great ones. One reason we're up so late is that I was telling the family all about the dragon boys. Kept a Candy Red up a whole week past his bedtime."

"Maybe we can read *Dragon Drums* next time," Charlie said. "Or *Where the Red Fern Grows*."

"Or both," said Nathaniel. "I'll be there right after Memorial Day."

"*Pipe down!* We want a little sleep!"

"Yeah!" sounded in a chorus around the wagon.

"It's a long fly home," Charlie whispered. "I'd better go."

"I guess so." Nathaniel yawned. "Sorry," he mumbled.

Charlie drifted up to the shutter and pulled it open. The balloons bumped gently around the walls. He scrambled through and sat on the sill. "Nathaniel? Would you answer just one more question?"

"Sure, Charlie." He dangled by Charlie's head.

"What's a group of balloons called?"

"A pride."

"I thought that was just for lions."

"Humph!" Nathaniel snorted. "Have you ever seen anything more proud than forty-seven-eleven balloons, all fat and sassy, sleek and glossy, straining to get to the sky?"

Charlie grinned. "You're right," he said. "I can't see why I didn't guess."

Nathaniel yawned again. "Most fair balloons sound more like a gaggle to me. Geese, you know. They talk a lot."

"Pipe down!"

"Good night, Nathaniel." He dropped to the ground.

"Good night, Charlie. See you after Memorial Day."

108

12

Grounded

Charlie stared at the closed shutter. He could hardly believe it. "Me," he said. "Me—Charlie Duncan—part of a pride."

A door banged on the other side of the camp.

Charlie jumped and headed back the way he'd come. He didn't feel like a member of a pride; he just felt cold.

The temperature had dropped fifteen degrees, and the snow fell thickly, silently, swiftly. He tried swimming a few steps, but it didn't work. Trying to puff your cheeks out while your teeth are chattering is impossible. And his arms and

109

legs were stiff. That general and his horse hadn't been a pile of pillows.

By the time Charlie trotted back into town and found the bus depot, he was colder than ice cream. He climbed aboard his bus and dropped into the seat behind the driver. "Bus fares are ridiculous," he mumbled as he stuffed thirty-five cents back into his pocket. There went $4.40. But at least it was warm. The heater was under his seat.

He closed his eyes and rested his head on the window. As he thawed out, he dozed off. He was high over the meadow, cartwheeling with Sapphira. Mr. Brickle stood on a cloud and shouted, "More! More!" Brunhilda sniffed and humphed in italics. Sam curled his lip and waved his slingshot. "I got him, little boy! You'll have to buy another . . ." "Hey, Charlie!" yelled Kate. "Where's your uniform?"

Charlie sneezed. And came groggily awake.

It became a pattern: Doze, dream, sneeze. Doze, dream, sneeze. "Bless you," the bus driver said each time.

After what seemed like hours, Charlie's teeth began to chatter again. He was cold in spite of the heat pouring out from under him. "A good thing I didn't balloon home," he muttered. "I'd never have made . . . AHHH-CHOO!"

"All out," called the bus driver. "Bless you," he added.

"Thanks," Charlie said. But it sounded more like "Tangs."

It wasn't snowing as hard here as it had been in Weston Town. Big flakes just floated lazily down. Maybe it hadn't been snowing long, he hoped. There wasn't much snow piled up anywhere.

As he turned into his walk, his front door flew open and banged against the wall.

"Charles David Duncan! Is that you?"

Charlie dragged himself up the walk. "Yes, Mom. *Ahhh-choo!* It's me— I."

"You get in this house this minute! Do you know how late it is? Where have you been?

"You're soaked!" she accused him when she saw him in the light.

"Ah-ah-ah-choo! Ah-CHOOOO!"

"Into the tub with you, young man! Now!"

A while later Charlie slumped down in the tub. The hot bubbly water felt good. He moved his arms and legs slowly and tried to pretend they didn't ache. It's been a long day, he thought. He was almost asleep when Dad knocked on the door. "Come in," Charlie called.

Dad sat on the edge of the tub and said, "Well, Charlie?" The mug of cocoa he held out sent up a plume of steam.

Charlie reached for it and watched the marshmallow melting fizzily. What could he say? Where should he begin? He didn't want to talk about the Blue Sox. Or Sam. And he doubted that Dad would believe—not *really* believe—he was part balloon. Or that he'd been visiting a balloon.

"I was out," he said finally.

"I'm aware of that, Charlie. The question is, where? It wasn't the soccer field. When it started to snow, I went to pick you up, but some kid—Sam, I think—said you just never showed up. Why didn't you . . .?" Dad paused and shook his head. "We'll go into that later."

Sam said . . . Charlie swallowed hard, past something that tasted like anger. That liar!

"Kate said you'd cleaned out your hedgehog and were dressed for the arctic."

Dad stopped talking.

Charlie knew he was waiting for him to say

112

something, but he couldn't think of anything to say. He just sat there sipping his cocoa.

"Stop stalling, Charlie. Where did you go?"

"Oh . . . uh . . . around?"

"Around. Around where?"

"Weston Town."

"Weston Town! That's twenty miles from here! What did you do 'around' Weston Town?"

"Uh . . . nothing much."

Dad cocked an eyebrow.

Charlie scrunched down in the tub. He felt two inches high. He wasn't lying, but he wasn't telling the truth, either. He bit his lip. Nathaniel is right, he thought. Lying is the worst thing there is. I don't want to be *anything* like Sam.

"I went to find an old friend. I met some new ones too. They're very nice," he added, when Dad didn't say anything. Well, he thought, Sapphira was nice. And Hugo.

Dad still didn't say anything.

"My old friend said he'd visit. Probably in the early part of June. Right after Memorial Day. He can't come any sooner." Maybe, Charlie thought, it wouldn't sound so bad if his nose weren't all stuffed up. The *n*'s and *m*'s came out all mished.

114

"What's your friend's name, Charlie?"

"Nathaniel J. Green."

"Okay, Charlie." Dad shook his head and his voice changed. "You should have told us where you were going. You scared your mother half to death. Even Kate began to worry."

"Kate?" he squeaked.

Dad nodded. "Strange as it may seem. And that's to say nothing of me. I ought to string you up by your thumbs, but you know the rules. What's to do, Charlie?"

Charlie sipped at the cooling cocoa. The rule was: Set your own punishment. That's the way they did it in his family. When you did something wrong, *you* had to decide what you deserved. Charlie thought it would be much easier the way other people did it. "I guess I'd better be grounded. A month?"

"Three weeks, I think. Right up to Christmas vacation. No television. No movies. Straight home after school. No stopping by Mr. Brickle's."

Charlie nodded and slipped back down into the water. That wasn't exactly the kind of grounded he had in mind, but he'd do, or rather wouldn't do, all those things too. For the first time Charlie understood "grounded" down to his toes, which would be firmly planted on the ground. And after all, he thought, balloons hibernate in winter.

Charlie almost smiled at his own joke, but Dad cleared his throat and said, "You can go to soccer practice and the game. Games, if you get into the play-offs. But that's because others are depending on you.

"Which reminds me, Charlie. Why *didn't* you go to the game today?"

"I—I . . . That is, Sam . . . I mean, I . . ." Charlie shook his head and shivered. If only he could think before he explained!

Dad took the mug. "That water's cold, Charlie." He handed Charlie a towel. "I think there's more to this than your playing hooky from a game, but we'll let it go for now. You've never lied to me, Charlie. I don't want you to start now."

Charlie stood up—and wobbled. The towel weighed four hundred pounds. Dad caught him as his legs folded.

13

Part of a Pride

On Sunday evening Mom stared at a thermometer and said, "No school for you tomorrow, Charlie."

"But, Mom!" he howled. "I feel fine. Honest!"

"That's good," she said, shaking the thermometer down. "Tuesday you'll feel even better."

Charlie turned over and buried his head in the pillow. Mothers! he humphed. One little sniff, they whip out the thermometer and slap you into bed.

On Tuesday morning the snow had melted and it was almost warm. As Charlie walked to school, he decided Mom had been right. He did

117

feel better. Even if getting through Monday seemed to take weeks. He'd tried to read, but he couldn't concentrate. Only one thing occupied his mind: Sam. He was going to have to face Sam down. The sooner the better.

Mrs. Li made a big fuss over her new bulletin board—a bunch of paper balloons with yarn strings. She even read some of the words printed on them. "Rainbow," she said. "Fleet. Bouquet. Burst."

"That's mine," Joseph whispered to Charlie as Mrs. Li tapped a yellow balloon called "blizzard." "And 'burst' is Mark's. Even Girard came up with one—a 'festival' of balloons. Not bad, huh?"

Charlie nodded but kept his eye on Sam. Sam curled his lip and looked disgusted. Charlie tried to sit small.

Mrs. Li held up two paper balloons, a red and a green. "Twenty-six down, two to go. Have you thought of one yet, Sam?"

Sam threw Charlie a dirty look and said, "I don't see why you won't take a *bunch* of balloons."

"I told you yesterday, Sam. It's blah. Use some

118

imagination for a change. How about you, Charlie?"

"A bunch of balloons is a pride," he said.

"Not bad," whispered Mark.

"See, Sam?" said Mrs. Li. "Everybody uses bunch. But *pride*. Now, that's a good one. What color balloon do you want, Charlie?"

Charlie barely heard her. He'd done it again. If looks could kill, he'd be dead. Sam snorted and turned his back.

"Charlie?"

"The green one, I guess." It looked more like an Apple Green than a Jade, but at least it reminded Charlie of Nathaniel.

That was the last time Charlie opened his mouth all day. Every time Sam looked at him, he slumped farther down in his seat. Then he'd look up at that Apple Green balloon and sit up. *Pride.* He was part of a pride. I never knew it was so hard to be proud, he groaned to himself.

After what seemed years, the final bell rang. Sam was out the door first. Joseph, Mark, and Girard were on his heels. If I hustle, Charlie thought, I can still get Sam alone.

But he dropped his homework folder, tripped

119

over a chair, and had to search for his soccer shoes. They weren't where he'd left them. They were buried at the bottom of the lost-and-found box. *Sam,* Charlie thought as he slammed out the door.

He ran the two blocks to the soccer field in record time. Everyone was on the field. Except Sam. He was kneeling on the sidelines. His shoelace must have broken, Charlie thought. Or maybe not, he decided as Sam stood up and looked at him.

"I want to talk to you," Charlie panted.

"You're not wanted here, balloon boy." Sam planted a hand in the middle of Charlie's chest and shoved. "Bigmouth!"

Charlie stumbled back. His heart beat so fast, he was afraid everyone could hear it. He wanted to run away, to not have to deal with this, to— to fly away!

Fly away! That'll show Sam what a real balloon boy is! he thought. I'll join a circus. They'll have to *pay* to see me!

Charlie swallowed hard. Members of a pride don't run away; they stand their ground. "Sam," he said, taking a really deep breath. "If I have a big mouth, that makes yours whale sized."

"Oh yeah?"

"You lied about me," Charlie said quietly. "And you're going to tell Coach."

"Oh yeah?"

"If you don't, *you'll* be the biggest chicken in the school. Not me."

"Nobody calls me chicken!"

Charlie saw Sam's fist coming up, tried to duck, and walked right into it. It hurt, but Charlie stayed on his feet. He almost laughed. The general packed a bigger wallop than Sam. "That doesn't change anything, Sam. You're still going to tell Coach." He wiped his nose on his sleeve. "Cowards run away from hard things, Sam. If you run from this . . ." Charlie shrugged.

"You get out of here!" Sam yelled, and raised his fists.

"No. I won't run away. Not ever again."

Sam pulled back his arm.

"Trouble, boys?" It was Coach Tyler.

"No," said Sam. He walked toward the field. "Let's get this show on the road."

"Wait a minute, Sam," said Coach. "What's this all about?"

"Nothing," said Sam. "Charlie can't stay, that's all."

"That's not true!"

Charlie looked around to see who yelled. The whole team was lined up behind Sam. They were all staring at him. It was me, he thought.

Charlie cleared his throat. He didn't want to do this with an audience, but Sam hadn't left him any choice. "Coach? Sam has something to tell you."

Sam narrowed his eyes and curled his lip. What a dumb routine, Charlie thought. How could that have scared me?

Sam glanced around and saw that the team was behind him. He smiled. "I don't have anything to say. Charlie's just making noises."

Joseph stepped forward. "That's not true. We heard part of what Charlie said."

"You shut up!" Sam yelled. "Who's captain here anyway?"

"That's enough!" Coach snapped. "What's this all about?"

"Nothing," said Sam, pushing Joseph out of the way. "Let's play."

Mark stepped in front of him. "What lie did you tell about Charlie?"

"You know what a bigmouth Charlie is."

"So what?" said Joseph. His hands poked

around looking for a hiding place. He put them in his waistband. "So he asks dumb questions in class. What's that got to do with soccer?"

"Everything!" Sam yelled.

He looks trapped, Charlie thought.

"Charlie play— plays good soccer," Girard put in.

"Not as good as me! And I'm the captain! *I* say who plays!"

"Really, Sam?" Coach Tyler smiled a funny smile.

Everyone ignored him.

"Well, Sam?" said Joseph. "What did you say about Charlie?"

"It's none of your business!"

"Maybe," said Mark. "But we'd still like to know."

Sam glared from one face to the other. "It's all your fault!" he shouted at Charlie.

Charlie shrugged a little. "I didn't lie."

"You should've kept your mouth shut!"

"You're probably right," said Charlie. "I never meant us to have to do all those reports; I just wanted to know things. And I didn't want this," he waved at the team. "But . . ." He shrugged again. "You shouldn't have lied."

There was silence.

Joseph finally broke it. "I don't like people who lie about my friends." His hands snuck out of his waistband. "What lie, Sam?"

Sam shuffled his feet.

Joseph turned to Charlie. "What lie, Charlie?"

Charlie's stomach was in knots. He didn't want to do this! "He . . . he said I was sick. That I couldn't play. I wasn't."

"Thought so," said Mark.

Coach cleared his throat.

"Sure, Coach," said Joseph, as though he were answering a question. "We're almost finished." His hands winked out of sight again. He looked around at the team.

"I nominate Joseph for our new team captain!" yelled Mark. "All in favor . . ."

"*Aye!*" The Blue Sox voted as one.

Sam didn't say anything. He just walked away.

Or maybe, Charlie thought as he pulled off his regular shoes, he's running away.

14

Winners

After practice Joseph and Mark walked home beside Charlie.

"That was a disaster," moaned Mark. "What are we going to do? If we lose tomorrow, no play-offs."

"We'll get better," said Joseph.

Charlie sighed. He should have kept quiet. At least till after the game. Wouldn't he *ever* learn when to shut up? "I'm sorry," he said. "I guess I should've waited . . ."

"No way, Charlie," said Mark. "Like Joseph says, we'll get better. I hope. Sam's a good forward, but I don't like liars."

Joseph nodded. "I don't either. Mark and I knew something was wrong even before you stood up to him. We saw him talking to Mrs. Coach on Friday. Then you came and left in a hurry."

Charlie didn't want to ask, but he had to know. "Mrs. Coach said, *'The boys told her.'* Who, uh . . . ?" He couldn't finish.

Mark shook his head. "Not us, Charlie. Not anybody but Sam. You know Mrs. Coach; she wants to think we all do everything together.

"Anyway, Charlie, on Saturday we saw your dad come to pick you up," Mark went on. "If you'd been sick like Sam said, he wouldn't have."

"But if I'd waited . . ." Charlie began again.

"Don't worry about it, Charlie," said Joseph. "My dad says, 'You can't trust a liar—anytime, anywhere.' Look at the way Sam walked out on us. He didn't have to do that." His right hand snuck out of his pocket. "He could have apologized. That would have put an end to it. Right?"

Charlie nodded.

"Right," Joseph answered his own question. "Besides, Charlie, you really are good. I don't know what you were trying today, jumping around like you were, but if you go back to your regular game, I think we've got the play-off in our pocket. Here's where we turn off." Joseph punched Charlie lightly on the shoulder. "See you tomorrow."

Charlie watched until they were out of sight and then walked on. It was nice of them not to blame him, but he felt rotten. With Sam gone, they needed an edge. He'd tried using his balloon-ness, but it hadn't worked. The third time he'd fallen flat, he'd lain there on the grass staring up into the blue forever above him. He remembered that magical feeling of being part of the universe. And suddenly he understood that soccer wasn't important enough for magic. "Besides," he whispered to the sky, "I think it would be kind of cheating."

Charlie sighed. "Maybe it will be okay. Maybe Joseph is right. . . . Maybe I've got an aptitude for soccer, too."

"Going to sneak in today, Charlie Duncan?" Mr. Brickle was leaning against the door of his shop as usual.

Charlie shook his head. "I'm grounded, Mr. Brickle."

128

"Too bad. Thought you might need some hot cocoa."

"That would have been good."

"How are things going?"

"I don't know, Mr. Brickle. Sometimes I think pretty good, and then . . ."

"Must be better, though," said Mr. Brickle. "Saw you talking with people for a change."

"Friends," said Charlie. And suddenly he felt better. Joseph was right. Even without his balloon-ness, they had a chance at the play-offs. *We* have a chance, he thought—me and my friends.

Mr. Brickle nodded as though he'd heard Charlie thinking. "That's good," he said, and lifted an eyebrow. "Tell me something, Charlie Duncan. Were you flying the other day?"

Charlie took a deep breath and nodded. He'd had enough lies to last six lifetimes. "Yes, sir. I'm part balloon."

"Thought so," said Mr. Brickle. He pushed himself away from the wall. "Let me know when you're flying again, Charlie Duncan."

"I will. See you, Mr. Brickle."

Out of habit, Charlie counted fence boards. Weird, he thought. Mr. Brickle wasn't even sur-

prised about my being part balloon. You'd think most people . . .

He stopped. He slid back the loose board. And blinked. "It couldn't be," he muttered, and dropped the board back into place. Mr. Brickle couldn't be part balloon. Could he?

Charlie took a deep breath, puffed out his cheeks, and flew a few feet. Then he remembered he was grounded and walked on home.